Christmas Wonderland

Vilhelm Hansen

© 1981 by Carlsen if, Copenhagen

Published in the United States and simultaneously
in Canada by Joshua Morris, Inc., 431 Post Road East,
Westport, CT 06880. All rights reserved.

Printed in Denmark

ISBN: 0-88705-090-5

The Christmas month has started. Old father gnome pokes his head through the branches and shouts, "Happy Christmas. Come along with me to the land of the gnomes, and let's have lots of fun!"

The gnomes have their own postal service. Little mice make sure that all the cards and packages are delivered. One mouse is responsible for the air mail, but it isn't very smart to have a snail in charge of the express mail, is it?

These poor little mice! The big cat has gone to sleep on top of all the packages and what do you think will happen if they try to wake him up?

The gnomes are very clever at making Christmas presents. "This year the children will be really surprised," says father gnome while he paints a rocking horse. Those two children peeping through the window won't be all that surprised, will they?

Some of the gnomes are getting ready to go into town, to give the city children a Christmas treat. They fix up the old airplane.

It looks as if that big, fat pig will have to stay at home, otherwise the plane will never get off the ground.

At Christmas time we sing Christmas carols. The gnomes do too, and they also play the fiddle. The fiddle is out of tune, and the gnomes try to tune it, using a pair of pliers and an oil can. Maybe kicking the wood with clogs might help!

Here we are at the gnomes' Christmas market. They love buying and selling, and instead of money they pay with laughter and kindness. Just look what you can buy in the market. Hand-knitted socks, Jumping Jacks, Christmas decorations, newly laid eggs, clogs, and beautiful Christmas trees.

Out in the forest the snow is thick and soft. The animals can't always find food for themselves. The gnomes try to help their animal friends, so they bring lots of food. A sheaf of corn for the birds, carrots for the hares, and turnips for the deer. And of course nuts for the squirrels. And who do you think the sausages are for? Probably for the fox.

The gnomes think it must be cold to be a
snowman. "Here you are, a nice, hot cup of tea."
Oh dear, that wasn't a very good idea. Ice cream
would probably have been better.

Where are the gnomes going? They all look so busy and
excited. Are they going to the grand Christmas ball in
the barn?

Yes, that is exactly where they are going. The gnome band is playing, and the happy tunes invite everybody to come and dance and be happy. It's a bit uncomfortable to be in the way, when the big, fat pigs fall over!

The gnomes love to dance. Just watch them ice-dancing. Clogs are no good on the ice. And did the eggs, which were going to be used for the Christmas baking, all break?

The gnomes need flour for the Christmas baking. The miller gnome has milled the flour, and the gnomes take it home on a sled, followed by the animals who know just what the flour is for. They are looking forward to tasting the cookies.

The Christmas baking in the land of the gnomes is a great occasion. Butter, flour and many other good things are mixed together, and the dough is rolled out to make gingerbread men, hearts, and lots of other cookies. How tasty the cookies look, as they come out of the oven! Father gnome would like a taste, but he is not allowed, not until Christmas Eve.

The animals in the stable have to know it is Christmas too. The horse is groomed, ready to pull the sled to church on Christmas morning.

There are turnips for the cow, but first she has to be milked. The pig is so strong, that he helps to carry the heavy sacks.

The gnome children, like all other children, like
to get Christmas presents. They have written a
list, which is so long that Grandfather fell asleep
trying to read it.

These gnomes are trying to count the birds in the
tree. They can't remember all the names of the
birds. How many names do you know? Can you
count how many birds there are in the tree?

Mother gnome is playing the piano. The trouble is that she bangs too hard on the keyboard, and the piano falls to pieces. The flower vase falls on the head of one of the children. Poor father gnome thought he was going to have a quiet time with his newspaper and pipe.

It is time for the Christmas circus. Some of the gnomes perform tricks and the rest look on. All the performers are very clever, particularly the pig, who can balance on one front leg.

The mice would like to give the gnomes a surprise. They are making Christmas decorations, hearts and little baskets.

The marzipan pig has a big, red ribbon tied around it, and one little mouse can't resist having a nibble.

All gnomes love rice pudding, but it is not a good idea to fall asleep while you are cooking it. I wonder what mother gnome is dreaming of while the rice pudding is boiling all over the kitchen?

The pig, the goose, the cat and the mouse hope that mother gnome will sleep for a long time, because the rice pudding tastes so good!

Now the rice pudding is ready, and there is plenty
for everybody. The animals love it.

Before the gnomes celebrate their own Christmas party, they give a party for the animals in the forest. They decorate the prettiest tree they can find, and the animals dance around it. Then they have jelly doughnuts to eat, and, at last, they all have Christmas presents.

The gnomes have found a beautiful big fir tree for their own
Christmas tree. The snow is falling just as it should at
Christmas time.

At long last it is really Christmas. The Christmas star shines
brightly in the sky. We have to hurry home for a real, old-
fashioned gnome Christmas.

The ringing of the church bells can be heard all
over the village. The gnomes are sitting on the roof
of the church singing, but the people inside the
church can't hear them.

The kind farmer has put a large bowl of rice pudding up in the attic with wooden spoons for the gnomes. In the middle of the rice pudding he has put a big lump of butter. This is the gnome's favorite dish, but only on Christmas Eve do they have butter in their rice pudding.

When they have finished eating they hear a merry bell outside.

They all know that the gnome king has arrived. At the back of his sleigh are little gnomes tossing out presents for the gnomes and animals. The gnome king does not have time to stay. He still has a long way to go before he has given all the gnomes and animals their presents.